This edition published by Parragon Books Ltd in 2016
and distributed by

Parragon Inc.
440 Park Avenue South, 13th Floor
New York, NY 10016
www.parragon.com
Please retain this information for future reference.

Written by Margaret Wise Brown
Illustrated by Lisa Sheehan

Edited by Lily Holland
Designed by Kathryn Davies
Production by Rich Wheeler

ISBN 978-1-4748-5745-1

Printed in China

the Find it Book

PaRRagon

Bath · New York · Cologne · Melbourne · Delhi
Hong Kong · Shenzhen · Singapore

Find the **honey** and **plenty** of money.

Find the Owl and the Pussycat.

Find five little monkeys jumping on a bed

Find Jack Sprat,
who ate no fat.

Find the **hole** where a stitch in time saves nine.

Find Little Bo Peep's lost **sheep**.

Find the **wolf** in sheep's clothing.

Find the **little piggy**
that went to the market.

Find the **little piggy** that went
whee-whee-whee all the way home.

3 miles

Find the **crooked man** who walked a crooked mile.

1 mile

2 miles

Find the **cow** that jumped over the moon.

Find the **dish** that ran away with the **spoon**.

Find **Humpty Dumpty** sitting on a wall

Find the **mouse** that ran up the clock.

Find **Itsy Bitsy Spider**
climbing up the waterspout.

Find **Georgie Porgie**, pudding and pie.

Find the **child** who had her cake and ate it, too.

Find the twinkle, twinkle little star.

Find the **man in the moon.**

Find your **favorite!**